DINO RANCH

BLITZ BREAKS LOOSE!

WRITTEN BY **KIARA VALDEZ** ILLUSTRATED BY **SHANE CLESTER**

ISBN 978-1-338-69221-1

10 9 8 7 6 5 4 3 2 1   22 23 24 25 26

Printed in the U.S.A.   40

First printing 2022

BOOK DESIGN BY **SALENA MAHINA**

SCHOLASTIC INC.

It's never a boring day at Dino Ranch!

There are triceratops to be tamed, raptors to be wrangled, and plenty of exciting new adventures to be had.

The lasso-swinging Cassidy family can solve any problem alongside their dino-partners! But sometimes, finding your dino-partner is not as easy as you might think...

Our story takes place just a little while ago. For one little rancher, things aren't too hunky-dory. Jon is looking mighty upset.

"What's wrong?" Min asks from on top of her gentle brontosaurus, Clover.

Miguel rides by on his tiny-but-mighty triceratops, Tango. "Yeah. What're you kicking your boots about?" he asks.

"I still don't have my dino-partner!" Jon says sadly.

"I tried petting pachycephalosauruses,

befriending parasaurolophuses,

and even making pals with stegosauruses. But nothing has worked!"

Jon opens his bag and reveals a dinosaur egg. "Ma, Pa, and you two have your dino-partners, and all I have is this egg I found this morning," Jon says.

The egg moves slightly, and a thin crack the ranchers hadn't noticed starts to widen.

"I think it's hatching," Miguel cheers.

First comes the stubby red nose and then the bumpy head of a baby velociraptor.

The tiny dino takes a quick look at the Cassidy siblings. Then, in the blink of an eye, he hops off Jon's lap and runs away.

"Suffering saddle horns! He's fast!" Jon says.

Jon looks around the corral and spots the baby all the way on the other side. "He's over there!"

10

The Cassidy kids hurry to catch the tiny dino, but he always manages to give them the slip.

Jon even tries to lure him with a treat! But no matter what Jon does, the baby velociraptor keeps his distance.

"Think fast!" Min yells, and a treat comes flying across the corral. The baby velociraptor dashes after the treat, happily catching it in his mouth.

"Whoa! The pterodactyl really flung his treat!
But that baby likes playing catch," Min says.

"Min, you are a genius!" Jon says. "I need to
show this baby velociraptor that I can *think*
fast, just like him!"

"But how are you going to do that?" Min asks. "We're much slower than him."

"I'm going to help him," Miguel says, patting Jon's shoulder.

"You are?" Jon says, a little confused.

"Yes, I am! There is nothing a little dino-might can't solve!" Miguel exclaims.

And so the Cassidy siblings get to work.

Jon and Min
pad the barn wall
with lots of hay
to provide a soft
landing for the
little dino.

Miguel builds his
new invention.

Jon puts on the safety gear and gets ready for action.

"All set!" Miguel says.

Min, Miguel, and Jon get into position.

Min waves the treat around in the air to get the baby velociraptor's attention. Then she flings it toward the barn wall!

At that moment, Miguel, Tango, and Clover tug on a rope.

Jon zooms off in the direction of the treat!

The little speedster was fast, but thanks
to Miguel's invention, Jon was faster!

Jon stretches his arm to grab the treat, and the baby velociraptor's mouth just misses it.

Jon grabs the treat first, but the baby velociraptor bumps into him at full speed.

CRASH!

They both fall and land in the hay.

"So you're fast *and* strong!" Jon says with a laugh. He pats the baby velociraptor on the head. "Let's name you Blitz."

Everyone can find their special dino-partner. It's all about connecting on the same level—or speed!